LAST STOP ON MARKET STREET

WORDS BY
MATT DE LA PEÑA

PICTURES BY
CHRISTIAN ROBINSON

G. P. Putnam's Sons • An Imprint of Penguin Group (USA)

For Luna and her two grandmas,
Roni and Grace
—M. de la P.

For Nana
—C. R.

CJ pushed through the church doors,
skipped down the steps.

The outside air smelled like freedom,

but it also smelled like rain,

which freckled CJ's shirt and dripped down his nose.

He ducked under his nana's umbrella, saying,

"How come we gotta wait for the bus in all this wet?"

"Trees get thirsty, too," his nana told him.

"Don't you see that big one drinking through a straw?"

CJ looked for a long time but never saw a straw.

From the bus stop, he watched water pool on flower petals.

Watched rain patter against the windshield of a nearby car.

His friend Colby climbed in, gave CJ a wave,

and drove off with his dad.

"Nana, how come we don't got a car?"

"Boy, what do we need a car for? We got a bus that breathes fire, and old Mr. Dennis, who always has a trick for you."

The bus creaked to a stop in front of them.
It sighed and sagged and the doors swung open.

"What's that I see?" Mr. Dennis asked.

He pulled a coin from behind CJ's ear,

placed it in his palm.

Nana laughed her deep laugh and pushed CJ along.

They sat right up front.

The man across the way was tuning a guitar.

An old woman with curlers had butterflies in a jar.

Nana gave everyone a great big smile

and a "good afternoon."

She made sure CJ did the same.

The bus lurched forward and stopped,
lurched forward and stopped.
Nana hummed as she knit.
"How come we always gotta go here
after church?" CJ said.
"Miguel and Colby never have to go nowhere."

"I feel sorry for those boys," she told him.

"They'll never get a chance to meet Bobo

or the Sunglass Man.

And I hear Trixie got herself a brand-new hat."

CJ stared out the window feeling sorry for himself.

He watched cars zip by on either side,

watched a group of boys hop curbs on bikes.

A man climbed aboard with a spotted dog.

CJ gave up his seat. "How come that man can't see?"

"Boy, what do you know about seeing?" Nana told him.

"Some people watch the world with their ears."

"That's a fact. Their noses, too," the man said, sniffing at the air.

"That's a mighty fine perfume you're wearing today, ma'am."

Nana squeezed the man's hand and laughed her deep laugh.

Two older boys got on next.

CJ watched as they moved on by and stood in back.

"Sure wish I had one of those," he said.

Nana set down her knitting.

"What for? You got the real live thing sitting across from you.

Why don't you ask the man if he'll play us a song?"

CJ didn't have to.
The guitar player was already
plucking strings
and beginning to sing.

"To feel the magic of music,"
the blind man whispered,
"I like to close my eyes."
Nana closed hers, too.

So did CJ and
the spotted dog.

And in the darkness,
the rhythm lifted CJ out of the bus,
out of the busy city.

He saw sunset colors swirling over crashing waves.
Saw a family of hawks slicing through the sky.
Saw the old woman's butterflies
dancing free in the light of the moon.
CJ's chest grew full and he was lost in the sound
and the sound gave him the feeling of magic.

The song ended and CJ opened his eyes.

Everyone on the bus clapped,

even the boys in back.

Nana glanced at the coin in CJ's palm.

CJ dropped it in the man's hat.

"Last stop on Market Street,"
Mr. Dennis called.

CJ looked around as he stepped off the bus.
Crumbling sidewalks and broken-down doors,
graffiti-tagged windows and boarded-up stores.
He reached for his Nana's hand.
"How come it's always so dirty over here?"

She smiled and pointed to the sky.

"Sometimes when you're surrounded by dirt, CJ,

you're a better witness for what's beautiful."

CJ saw the perfect rainbow arcing over their soup kitchen.
He wondered how his nana always found beautiful
where he never even thought to look.

He looked all around them again,
at the bus rounding the corner out of sight
and the broken streetlamps still lit up bright
and the stray-cat shadows moving across the wall.

When he spotted their familiar faces in the window, he said,
"I'm glad we came."

He thought his nana might laugh
her deep laugh, but she didn't.
She patted him on the head and told him,
"Me too, CJ. Now, come on."